The Goblins Giggle
and other stories

The Goblins Giggle
and other stories

Selected and illustrated by Molly Bang

CHARLES SCRIBNER'S SONS, NEW YORK

To Ed and Namhi Wagner

"The Old Man's Wen"
is translated and adapted from "Kobutori," in
Yuzuru, Hikoichibanashi, by Junji Kinoshita.

Contents

The Old Man's Wen

There was once an old man who had a lump on his cheek called a wen. It was on his right cheek and it was big, so big that it got in the way when he ate, and he had to eat with his left hand. He couldn't see his right foot to put on his right shoe, it was so big. And of course he had to sleep with his left side down, which is most unlucky.

When he walked on the street people turned to stare at him; children tried to trip him and make him fall. The old man grew so unhappy that at last there were only two things he liked to do. One was to dance with his family; he danced with his wife, he danced with his children, and he danced with his grandchildren. He even danced alone. He danced to ballads and marches and lullabies, to sea chanteys, work tunes, gay tunes, and dirges. He danced when there was no music at all, to tunes inside his head.

The other thing the old man liked to do was to take long walks by himself in the mountains. As he climbed the steep paths or went down into the valleys, he hummed to himself and forgot his sorrow.

One day he was out walking when the sky suddenly grew dark and a fierce wind howled down from the peak of the mountain. Black clouds gathered and covered the treetops; the clouds opened, and hard chill rain fell on the forest. The old man quickly looked about for shelter.

Right before him, he saw an old tree with a big hole in the base of it, just big enough for him to sit in and keep dry. He climbed in and pulled his knees up against his chest, then looked out at the water falling in the forest. The wind howled louder, the rain fell harder. The air grew bitter cold.

The old man's teeth began to chatter and his body began to shake. He pulled his knees tight under his chin and huddled into a ball. Night came, but the wind still howled and the rain still fell.

"Oh, how I would like to be home in my nice warm bed," the old man thought. "Lying in bed on my unlucky side is luckier than this."

Soon his head fell onto his knees and his eyelids closed over his eyes.

"Oh! I fell asleep!" he said, as he opened his eyes many hours later. The wind had stopped howling; the rain no longer fell. There was peace in the night woods. The old man poked his head out of the hole. Ah! High above, the moon was out. In the still blue night, deep in the forest, the round full moon was shining. The old man looked up at it and smiled.

TWO

He started to crawl from the hole, but when he got half-way out, he thought he heard voices, voices of a crowd of people. "Maybe I'm still asleep," he thought, and he pinched himself to be sure. The voices only got louder, filling the air. Then black shapes moved toward him from the trees. One by one they came, chattering and cackling. Closer they moved, and closer, until right there in front of the hole in the tree, the creatures all sat down.

The old man squeezed against the back of the tree and shook with fear. He was curious though, even more curious than he was scared. He peeked out again. Dozens and dozens of creatures were there, sitting in front of the tree. He couldn't make out their faces until they suddenly lifted them to the moon, raising their voices in a single scream:

Eeeeeeeeeeeeeeeeeeeeeeeeeah!

The old man shrank into the back of the hole. Goblins! He shivered. He shook. He cautiously peeked out again. Some of them had mouths in the back of their heads, some had eyes all over their faces, and some had twisted horns. There were some with feet like the claws of birds, and some covered over with scales. One who sat nearest the hole was grinning; his sharp teeth glowed green in the moonlight. The old man couldn't run, and he couldn't yell for help, so he sat and watched and held his breath.

The goblins were having a party! Curious bottles and little cups were brought out, and the goblins began to drink.

The biggest and ugliest was obviously the boss. He sat on a pillow embroidered with purple and gold; his cup was enormous and looked like a misshapen mushroom.

The goblins drank and cackled for a time in goblin gibberish; then one little creature jumped up and danced. Another jumped up, then another, and so they all jumped up and danced. They beat the ground and slapped their knees; they sang with voices like broken brass horns. So loud and awful the racket was that the old man covered his ears.

But he soon got curious again. He uncovered his ears and poked his head out of the hole to see. There was the boss goblin in the middle of them all, waving his hairy arms about and shaking his head full of horns.

"Dance a better dance!" he roared. "Sing a better song!" The goblins turned somersaults and jumped in the air, and this is what they sang:

Dumm dumm dumm dumm
Skree skree skraaaagh
Kackle Kackle
Kickle Kockle
Eeeeeeeeeeeeeeeeeeeee!

"What a terrible song," thought the old man. He pushed himself halfway out of the hole to see better. The goblins danced up and they danced around and they danced until they fell down. Then they got up and danced again. The old man's feet began to dance too, down in the hole in the tree.

He wanted to dance, he wanted to sing, but his fear of the goblins held him back. The goblins went on dancing.

Dumm dumm dumm dumm
Skree skree skraaaagh

The old man's hands started clapping to the song; his feet danced out from under him.

Kackle Kackle
Kickle Kockle

Suddenly his body leaped from the tree hole! Smack in the midst of the goblins he landed, right in front of the goblin boss!

Eeeeeeeeeeeeeeeeeeeee!

He danced from his head to the ends of his toes, from his toes back up to his head. He twirled and whirled; he jumped and he thumped; he wiggled his head and waggled his nose. The goblins laughed. They clapped. They sang another song.

Monday, Tuesday, Wednesday, Thursday, they sang.
Monday, Tuesday, Wednesday, Thursday.

"That's a dreadful song," the old man thought, "and anyway, they didn't sing the end."

Friday! he yelled out.

Monday, Tuesday, Wednesday, Thursday, sang the goblins.
Monday, Tuesday, Wednesday, Thursday!

Friday! sang out the old man.

SEVEN

The boss of the goblins clapped his hands. He stomped his feet and his belly jiggled with laughter.

Monday, Tuesday, Wednesday, Thursday! he roared.

Monday, Tuesday, Wednesday, Thursday! sang the goblins.

Friday! sang out the old man.

Suddenly, quiet.

"What happened?" the old man wondered. All was still. Then from far, far, far away he heard the crow of a rooster. It was dawn. The dozens and dozens of goblins turned their heads to the lone old man. The goblin boss moved toward him. Silently the goblins moved with him and came to stand in circles around the old man. No one spoke. No sound. They set their pale eyes on the old man's face.

Quiet as quiet it was, and he was scared as scared. Scared to stay and scared to run, he bowed his head between his shoulders and looked at his trembling knees.

"Grampa!" roared the goblin boss.

The old man could not answer.

"Grampaaaa!" he roared again. "Year upon year we have danced in these woods, but never have we had such a dance as tonight."

"He's pleased!" the old man thought, and his knees trembled less.

"Grampa, Grampaaa," growled the boss of the goblins. "Come back and dance with us again. You must come again!"

In a voice tinier than a flea's, the old man answered.

"Yessir," he squeaked. "I'll come." But he knew in his heart that he would never come near this place again, not if he lived to three hundred and seven. He looked at his knees and thought of his breakfast and his family.

But now out of the circle slipped a goblin, a goblin with two scaley tails growing out of his skinny green arms. He bowed low to his boss and spoke with a sickly sweet whine.

"Grampa must come back to us, Your Excellency," he simpered, "but how can we make sure?"

He slithered over to the old man. "How can we be sure, Grampa?" he whispered in his face, and his breath smelled of wine and rotten teeth.

The other goblins began to yell. "How can we make sure?" they screamed. "How can we make sure?"

"Let's take something away from him, the thing he prizes most."

"Yes, we'll take it and keep it until he comes back!"

"Ho!" thundered the boss of the goblins. "We'll take his lump, we'll take his wen! That's the only mark of beauty he has!"

The old man shook until he almost fell down. Closer the goblins came, and their claws reached out for the wen. The old man covered it with both hands, but the goblins reached for his hands.

"No!" the old man cried. "This is my only treasure! Don't take it away!"

ELEVEN

Closer the goblins moved, and their claws closed over his fingers. They pulled his hands away; more claws reached out for the wen. He shut his eyes and fainted dead away.

When the old man opened his eyes, the sun was shining. The goblins were gone. He got up from the ground and stretched, his legs stiff and his joints cracking. He put his hand up to the wen.

It wasn't there! None of it! Nothing but a wrinkled cheek, exactly like the other. The old man jumped and laughed and sang and ran down the mountain to his family.

The Boy Who Wanted to Learn to Shudder

There was once a couple whose son was strong and healthy but dullwitted. There were countless everyday things he couldn't understand. When there was anything to be done the parents had to do it themselves, because it took the son longer to understand how to do it than it did to do the work itself. But if it was dark and there was something to fetch on the other side of the graveyard or in the dark woods, the couple would put off the task for another day. "It makes me shudder!" they would say.

When scary stories were told late at night, the guests would huddle together and their eyes would grow wide as they listened.

"Oh! It makes me shudder!" they would whisper to each other.

The son sat in a corner and wondered what they could mean. " 'It makes me shudder! It makes me shudder!' they always say, but I don't shudder at all," he thought. "That must be something else I'll have to learn."

One day the boy's father spoke to him. "Son," he said, "you are big, and it's time you learned something to earn your own bread by."

"Well, Father," he answered, "I'd be quite happy to do that. Could you teach me how to shudder?"

The father scratched his head and stared at his fool of a son. "You'll learn how to do that easily enough," he said, "but it will earn you no bread."

Several days later the sexton came to visit, and the father complained to him about his witless son. "Imagine!" he said. "Only the other day I asked him how he expected to earn his bread, and he answered that he wanted to learn to shudder!"

"Oh, that'll be easy to teach him," answered the sexton. "Just send him to live with me for a while."

Next day, the father sent his son off to live with the sexton. The sexton set him to ringing the church bells, and taught him in less than a week.

"Now I'll teach him to shudder," said the sexton to himself, and he told the boy to ring the bells at midnight. That night the boy trotted up the stairs to ring the bells. The sexton had secretly gone before him, with white cream on his face and hands, his hair all full of white powder.

Just as he turned to take hold of the bell rope, the boy saw a ghostly figure across from the sounding hole.

SIXTEEN

"Who are you?" the boy asked politely, but the figure made no reply.

"Answer," said the boy, "or go away. You have no business here at this time of night."

The sexton stood stock still and silent, so the boy would think he was a ghost, but the boy cried out, "Who are you? Speak up or I'll throw you down the stairs."

"He can't really mean that," thought the sexton, and stood silent as a stone. The boy warned him once more, but when he got no reply, he threw the ghost down the bell tower steps and left him in a heap in the corner. He rang the bells as he had been told and went back to the sexton's house to bed.

The sexton's wife waited and waited for her husband to return. Finally she went to the boy's bedroom and woke him up.

"Do you know where my husband is?" she asked. "He climbed up the bell tower just before you."

"No, I don't," replied the boy. "I saw someone with hands and face like white pasty cream and hair like cotton fuzz, standing across the sounding hole, but he wouldn't answer when I spoke or go away when I said to. I thought he must be there for some evil and threw him down the stairs."

The woman ran to the tower, followed by the boy, and there she found her husband in a heap in the corner, moaning over a broken rib.

The boy saw the unhappiness he had caused and went home to his father to tell him what had happened.

SEVENTEEN

"Only wait until it's daylight," the boy went on. "I'll go out and learn to shudder, so I'll have at least one skill to earn my bread by."

Next morning, the boy set out. His parents were sorry to see someone so stupid go out with nothing at all, so they gave him fifty silver pieces and a big loaf of pumpernickel bread with cheese for his lunch.

The boy said good-bye and set off down the road. He walked all day, and at nightfall he came to an inn. The boy took a room on the second floor and came down for supper in the dining room.

As he cut his hot sausage and poured sauce on his potatoes, he muttered to himself, "If only I could learn to shudder. If only I could learn to shudder."

The innkeeper heard him and laughed.

"If that's what you want," he said, "there is a place nearby where you are quite certain to learn."

"Hush!" cried his wife. "Too many people have already been lost inside. Why send in another, especially when he is young?"

But the boy insisted. "If it will teach me to shudder, then I must go, because that's the reason I left home." He pressed the innkeeper so much that at last he gave in.

"Not two miles down the road from here is a haunted castle," the man said, "where no one has stayed for three nights and come out alive. The castle is said to contain great treasure, but it is guarded by evil spirits who kill all those trying to take it away. The king has promised half the king-dom to whoever can rescue the gold and jewels, but no one has succeeded, and many have lost their lives."

The boy went straight to the king next morning and said that he would be happy to spend three nights in the castle, if that would teach him how to shudder. The king was pleased and said, "You may ask for three things to take with you into the castle, but they must be things without life."

The boy thought and thought and finally asked for a fire, a turning lathe, and a cutting board with its knife. The king had these things taken into the castle for him that very day.

The sun was just setting behind the golden wheat fields when the boy walked through the gates of the haunted castle. He lit a blazing fire in the main hall, set the cutting board and knife on the hearth, and sat beside the turning lathe.

"Ah," he sighed, "if only I could learn to shudder. I'll certainly never learn it here."

Just before midnight, he began to poke the fire, when out of the darkness he heard two voices whining.

"How cold we are," they whimpered. "Oh, how cold we are."

"Well, come up to the fire and warm yourselves," said the boy.

Suddenly, there were two giant black cats on either side of him, glaring out with fiery eyes. After a short time they were warm enough.

TWENTY

"Would you like to play cards?" one suggested.

"Why not?" the boy answered. "But let me see your paws first."

"Oh, what long claws you have!" he exclaimed. "Here, let me cut them for you." He grabbed them by their necks, turned them onto the cutting board, and chopped off their monstrous heads.

As soon as he returned to his fire, black dogs jumped out of the shadows. They tore apart his fire and swallowed the coals, then breathed flames in his face.

"This is too much!" the boy cried, and he slashed about with the cutting knife until all were dead or chased away. Then he pulled the fire together again and slept.

When the king found him lying there next morning, he thought he was dead.

"What a pity for one to die so young," he sighed.

The boy heard and jumped to his feet.

"I'm not nearly dead," he told the king, "but I haven't learned how to shudder."

The second night he returned to the fireplace in the castle and sat by the flames wishing he could learn how to shudder, when a great drowsiness fell on him and he bowed his head in sleep. At midnight he awoke to the sound of thunder up in the chimney. Boom! Boom! Boom! Closer and closer it rolled, then suddenly half a man fell out into the fire and tumbled beside him on the hearth.

"This isn't enough," said the boy. "Where's the rest of you?"

No sooner had he spoken than the rumbling came again, louder, closer, until the other half fell out and joined the rest of itself, forming a hideous man.

The boy went to stoke up the fire, but when he turned round, he saw that the man had taken his seat on the stool. The intruder raised his horny hand and boxed the boy on his ear. The boy pushed him off onto the floor.

"I'll thank you to find your own seat," said the boy, and sat down.

Rumbling was heard in the chimney again, and one by one nine men fell out, each uglier than the last. With them they carried nine leg bones and two skulls, to play at ninepins with.

"Could I play with you?" the boy asked.

"Yes, if you have any money."

"Money enough," said the boy, "but the balls are not quite round." He took the skulls and turned them on the lathe until they were round as bubbles. They played for a while, and he lost four pieces of silver, but at cock crow they all disappeared, and the boy went to sleep once more by the fire.

When the king came to see how the boy had done, he answered that he had had a wonderful night playing at ninepins, but he still had not learned to shudder.

The third night, there he was once more in front of the fire, wishing he could learn how to shudder, when into the hall walked an old, old, bearded man. He was uglier still than he was old, and meaner than he was ugly.

"You fool!" he cackled. "You'll know very soon what it is to shudder, for I am going to kill you!"

"Perhaps not," answered the boy, "for I think I am as strong as you and maybe stronger."

"We shall see," said the ghost, and led him downstairs.

Deep under the castle they went, through dark passages covered with mold and slime, until they came to a smith's forge. The old man took an ax and with one blow struck an anvil into the ground.

"I can do better than that," said the boy, and went to the other anvil, followed by the old man, who stood beside him to watch.

The boy quickly turned and grabbed the old man's beard, set it across the anvil, and wedged it in with one blow of the ax, so the old ghost was caught.

"Mercy!" he cried. "Have mercy, and I'll show you the treasures of the castle!"

The boy let him go and followed him to a cellar where there stood three chests full of gold.

"One of these is for the poor," the old man told him, "one is for the king, and the last is for yourself." He turned and walked out the door and was never seen again.

The boy felt his way back to the main hall, through the

passages of slime, and went to sleep in the front of the fire. The king came next morning, along with the queen and their beautiful daughter.

"Good morning," said the boy. "I talked last night with a bearded man who showed me chests full of gold, but I still haven't learned how to shudder."

The princess thought this so funny that she decided to marry him on the spot, and of course he consented.

They lived happily for several years, but the young man was still troubled. Even when things were gayest, a cloud would suddenly cover his face, and he would set to grumbling.

"If only I could learn to shudder. If only I could learn to shudder."

His wife finally became fed up with his foolishness and decided to teach him herself.

She had her waiting-maid go down to the stream in the garden and bring back a bucket full of minnows. That night when the prince was sound asleep, she drew the covers off him and emptied the bucket full of cold water and fish onto him. He jumped up shivering and shuddering, and stuttered through his chattering teeth, "Ah w-w-w-wonderful w-w-w-w-w-ife, you have f-f-f-inally t-t-t-t-aught me to sh-sh-sh-sh-sh-sh-sh-udder!"

Mary Culhane
and the Dead Man

There once was a girl named Mary Culhane, who lived with her family on the other side of the graveyard. One day her father rested a while in the graveyard on his way back from town, leaving his blackthorn walking stick near a new-dug grave. It was only at supper that he remembered it.

"What's wrong, husband?" asked Mrs. Culhane.

"I'm afraid I left my blackthorn stick in the graveyard," he said, "just by the new-dug grave. I hope no gypsies steal it in the night, for it's a prize shillelagh."

The children looked at one another, thinking of the haunted tombs, then looked down at their plates. Mary Culhane alone stood up.

"I'll get it," she said, and before her parents could stop her, she walked out the door into the black, black night.

It was a while before she came to the new-dug grave and saw her father's blackthorn shillelagh, a black strip on the gray-black graveyard grass. As she reached out her hand for it, a hoarse voice came from out of the grave.

"Leave the blackthorn, Mary Culhane, and help me out of this hole."

Mary shook and Mary trembled, but a power took hold of her and drew her toward the voice.

"Take the lid off the casket," the hoarse voice whispered. Her hands took the lid off, all unwilling, and her eyes looked down on the dead man inside.

"Take me up on your back," he hissed. Her arms wouldn't move, so the dead man climbed up himself. Then away from the new-dug grave she walked, with the dead man on her back pointing the way. His fingers were clammy, cold about her neck, and the dead weight of him hung heavy on her back. She walked a mile but could go no more.

The wet white fingers closed about her neck.

"Walk on, Mary Culhane," said the corpse, and Mary Culhane walked on. Half a mile on they came to a village, where the houses stood side by side.

"Take me to the first house," said the dead man. She took him.

"We can't go in," he said. "I smell the smell of clean water, but I smell the smell of holy water, too."

She took him to the next house.

"We can't go in," the corpse whispered. "I smell clean water, but holy water as well."

She took him to the third house.

"Go in here," he said. "There's no clean water in this house, but there's no holy water either."

They went inside, and Mary put the dead man on a chair by the hearth.

"Find me something to eat and drink," he ordered. She found a dish of oatmeal and brought it to him.

"There is nothing to drink but dirty water," she said.

"Bring me a dish and a razor."

She found a dish and a razor and brought them.

"Come, now," he said, "to the room upstairs."

She carried him up to the room, where three young men lay sleeping in bed. The dead man made a cut on the finger of each young man, and three drops of blood from each fell into the dish. When the first drop fell, their breathing stopped; the second fell and the flush went from their faces. After the third drop fell, they were white and cold as the corpse himself.

"That's for leaving no clean water," he whispered. Mary carried him back downstairs.

The dead man mixed the oatmeal with the blood of the three young men, divided it in two, and told the girl to get two spoons, which she did.

"Eat," said the corpse, and proceeded to gobble his own portion.

Mary Culhane removed the kerchief from her head and tied it around her neck like a scarf. Then, pretending to spoon the food into her mouth, she dropped it all into her kerchief instead.

"Are you finished?" asked the dead man, licking his pale lips.

"I am," said Mary Culhane.

"Then take me back to where you found me, and be quick."

Mary quaked at leaving the house again, but her limbs moved once more against her will. Slow as she could she cleared off the dishes. Afraid that the dead man would smell the oatmeal in her kerchief, she untied it from her neck when her back was to him. Quickly she rolled it up and hid it in the cupboard.

The dead man ordered her back a shorter way, through the fields. Slow as she could she walked, with the dead weight hanging down.

"Is there any cure for those three young men?" she asked.

"There is none," the corpse laughed, "for we've eaten it up. If one bit of that food had been put in each man's mouth, they would have come alive and never known of their deaths. But the food is swallowed down, and they are dead."

They walked on, and the dead man pointed to three piles of stones.

"There is a pot full of gold under each of those," he said. "None knows of it except the dead." Mary wondered at this, for she wasn't dead, but she walked on in silence.

On and on she carried him, until at last they came to the wall of the graveyard. Suddenly the girl heard a cock crowing, far off in the valley.

"The cock is crowing," she cried. "I should be going home."

"That's not a cock," the dead man whispered, "but only the hoot of an owl. Hurry on."

She carried him inside the graveyard, deathly tired and with her back nearly breaking. Slowly, slowly she walked with him through the gravestones.

Again she heard the crow of a cock.

"That's no bird," wheezed the dead man. "It's only a lamb that is lost from its mother."

But Mary Culhane felt him shiver as he spoke. Slower she went.

"Hurry on!"

Slower still she walked.

At last they came to the mouth of the grave; the black hole gaped wide.

"Now, my lovely girl," the dead man cackled, "it's into the grave with you!"

His dead arms pulled her down with him; dead fingers clutched at her living flesh. Slowly, surely, he drew her down.

Just at that moment, the cock crowed for the third time, and the fingers relaxed and fell, powerless. The dead man dropped into his coffin alone.

"Ah, Mary Culhane," the dead man sighed, and his words were no more than faint wheezes, "if I had thought the cock would crow before I was in the grave, I would never have told you of the gold."

He closed his eyes and fell silent.

The girl folded his hands across his chest and settled him carefully, then shut the coffin lid tight behind her. She picked up her father's blackthorn shillelagh from the ground and walked home.

The sky was pale gray by the time Mary Culhane unlatched her front door. No one was awake. She set the stick by the hearth and fell fast asleep as soon as she touched her bed, weary in all her bones.

In the middle of the morning she woke up to her mother's rough shaking.

"Lazy girl," she scolded, "you sleep all morning, and here the three sons of our neighbors have died in their beds. Get up, get up! We have to attend their wake."

"Go without me then," said Mary, "for I am sick from weariness." Her mother then saw that she was pale as the sheets. She covered her again and left with her husband and the other children.

Mary Culhane awoke at noon. She rose out of bed, drank a bowlful of fresh milk warmed on the stove, and ate a large slice of bread with honey. Then she set off for the neighbor's house.

When she arrived she found a great crowd of people, all wailing and shaking their heads. She looked for the parents of the three young men and found them sobbing and wringing their hands.

"There's no need to cry," she said to them.

The parents looked at her, unbelieving. "No need to cry, you heartless girl, with our three fine sons dead in their beds!"

"What would you give," asked Mary Culhane, "to whoever could bring them back to life?"

"It's no time for joking," cried the father, and turned away in his sadness.

"I'm not joking, or teasing you either," said the girl. "I can bring them back to life, but I want the field with the three stone heaps for my work."

"You are welcome to that and more," the parents said, "but our sons are dead."

"Give me the field in handwriting," she said.

The parents gave her the field in handwriting. Mary Culhane then asked that everyone leave the house. The crowd took her for mad, but they walked out the door.

Mary took the kerchief from where she had hidden it in the cupboard. She walked upstairs and put three bites of the oatmeal and blood in the mouths of each of the three young men. At the first bite, their bodies became warm. With the second, the color returned to their faces, and with the third bite they were breathing, deep asleep.

The girl opened the door and called the people inside.

"Wake up your sons," she said to the parents.

The parents called each son by name, and each son woke. They sat up and stared at the people standing about them. Mary Culhane then described what had happened the night before, though she mentioned nothing about the pots of gold.

THIRTY-NINE

The parents embraced their sons with joy and gave a big party to celebrate their return to life.

Mary received the field that was promised her. Before long, she dug up the gold and built a house for herself, with plenty of room for her parents and friends to visit.

It is also said that she married the eldest of the three sons and that they lived a long and happy life. But she was always sure to keep clean water and holy water in the house, and she never made oatmeal.

A Soccer Game on Dung-ting Lake

Wang Shir-shou was a young man so strong that he could lift a stone mortar weighing several hundred pounds. He and his father were both good at soccer and often practiced together in the courtyard.

When Wang was about thirty, his father had been out in a boat on Dung-ting Lake with friends. A sudden squall came up; the boat was sunk, and all on board were lost. Their bodies were never found.

Eight or nine years after this, Wang was on his way to a distant city and happened to reach Dung-ting Lake just after dusk. While the boatmen tied the boat to the moorings, they all watched the moon rise in the east, turning the water to a bright sheet of light.

Suddenly the surface was broken by ripples. Five men rose out of the lake and spread a large mat on the shining water. The boatmen were terrified and hid in the bottom of the boat, but Wang stayed where he was and watched.

Food and wine were set out on the mat in dishes of delicate porcelain. Wang saw the cups and bottles knock against each other; they didn't clink like ordinary dishes but made soft, hollow sounds.

Three of the men sat down on the mat. One was dressed in yellow robes, the other two in white; all wore black turbans on their heads. The seated men seemed grave and dignified as ancient sages, but by moonlight Wang could not make out their faces.

The two remaining men, who were serving them, were dressed all in black. One seemed quite young, almost a boy; the other was much older and reminded Wang of his father, though his voice was much lower and more melodious than he remembered.

Near midnight, one of the men suggested a game of soccer. The boy disappeared under the water and immediately returned with a huge silver ball that glowed from inside as though it were filled with silver phosphorescence.

All the men stood up. The man in yellow ordered the old attendant to join the game, and they kicked the ball about for a while. It seemed to shine brighter the higher it rose; when it rose twenty feet in the air it was so dazzling that it blinded Wang's eyes, then softened to a silver glow as it fell to the water.

Suddenly the ball was kicked toward Wang. It fell

into his boat, right beside him! Wang couldn't resist; he picked up the ball, drew back his foot, then kicked with all his might.

Much to his surprise, the ball was so soft and light he scarcely felt it. His foot broke through and went deep inside. The ball flew up, but as it rose a stream of light like a rainbow poured from the hole Wang had made. It fell and trailed behind it a blazing tail, like a comet rushing across the sky. It glided down to the water, where it flickered a moment and went out.

"Hey!" the players cried out. "What living creature dares to interrupt our game?"

But the old attendant praised Wang.

"Excellent kick!" he shouted over. "That's a favorite drop kick of my own!"

One of the men in white turned angrily on the old man.

"You withered carcass! How dare you joke when some human like yourself has ruined our game? Go with the boy and bring the man here, or you'll be beaten until your back is striped with blood!"

Wang had no way to escape. He stood and waited in the middle of the boat, his hand on his sword. The boy and the old man drew nearer; they too held swords. All at once, Wang saw that the old man really was his father!

"Father!" he cried out. "I'm your son!"

The old man was now afraid for his son, but his fear was mixed with joy at finding him again.

FORTY-THREE

Meanwhile, the boy had gone back and told the three men what had happened. Out of nowhere they appeared alongside the boat and jumped inside. Seen up close, their faces were scaley and black as tar; their eyes were big as pomegranates. Together the creatures went for the old man. Wang slashed at them and cut off the arm of the one in yellow, which dropped into the boat. The monster fled.

One of the two in white then charged at him. Wang struck; the frightful head flew off and splashed into the water, and the body fell in after it. The other creature saw what had happened and disappeared over the side.

Wang and his father set the boat loose from its moorings, anxious to escape. All at once a huge mouth rose out of the water, deep and wide as a mine-tunnel. The mouth was ringed with rows of pointed teeth. It belched out a violent gust of wind; the waves rose high as mountains.

The boatmen clutched each other in terror, but Wang seized one of the two enormous stones which were used on board as anchors. He threw it into the gaping mouth, which sank beneath the water. Wang threw in the second stone; the waves subsided and the lake became calm.

Wang thought his father must be a ghost, but the old man reassured him.

"I never died," he said. "There were nineteen of us who sank with the boat that day. The others were all eaten by the fish-goblins, but I was saved because I could play soccer. The three you saw were really creatures of the sea; they were

banished to this lake by the Dragon King. The ball they were playing with was the bladder of a deep-sea fish."

The boatmen rowed the two men across to shore, and they landed when dawn mists still covered Dung-ting Lake. As they climbed ashore, the father and son looked back into the boat. There on the bottom lay a fin as big as a table—it was the arm that Wang had cut off the night before.

The Goblins Giggle

Once upon a time there was an old couple who had a daughter whom they loved very much. At last it came time for the girl to be married. The bridegroom lived in a distant village, and on the wedding day he sent a fine palanquin to carry his bride to him over the mountains.

With her parents leading the way and all her friends and relatives parading behind, the girl was carried off toward her new home.

"The bride! The bride!" they yelled, as the procession marched down into the valley and on up the mountain. Just as they reached the mountaintop, a cloud black as coal dust appeared in the sky. Straight over to the wedding party it blew, and before anyone knew what had happened, it enveloped the palanquin and floated away with the girl inside.

The old couple went almost crazy with grief. They cried, they beat their chests, they tore their hair, but their daughter

did not come back. At last the mother decided to go look for her. Without a word to anyone, she put on her traveling clothes and set off.

The old woman walked until the sun was setting, when she noticed a little temple by the side of the road. Inside was a nun, her head shaved bare.

"Come in," she said kindly. "I have nothing to cover you with nor food to offer you, but you are welcome to sleep here if you wish."

The old woman was so tired that she lay down as soon as she was in the door. The nun took off her own robe and covered her guest, then spoke.

"The daughter you are looking for has been taken to the Goblin Mansion, just beyond the river. To get there, you must cross Abacus Bridge, which is guarded by two dogs. One dog is very big, the other very small, but both are fierce and feast on human flesh. It is only safe to cross at noon, for during that time they are asleep.

"The bridge itself is like a great abacus, but is strung with pearls instead of beads. You must be careful not to step on these or touch them, beautiful as they are. If you do, you will find yourself back in the village where you lived as a child."

Next morning the old woman awoke to the sound of soft rustling. There was no temple, no nun in sight; she lay alone in the middle of a wide field of *susuki* grass, which rustled in the morning breeze. Her pillow was a small stone marker, weathered by wind and rain; a layer of new-cut grass covered her like a blanket.

The woman silently thanked the nun for her advice and set out toward the river. She reached it just at noon. The dogs lay asleep on either side of the Abacus Bridge. The old woman tiptoed past them.

The pearls of the bridge gleamed white in the noonday sun, so smooth and pure that she almost put out her hand to touch them. But the words of the nun came swiftly to mind, and she drew back her hand.

Carefully she stepped onto the first rung, avoiding the pearls. Aieee! It was hot as a poker! She jumped to the next, the next, and the next. Her feet were burning; the white pearls dazzled her eyes. On she ran, half blinded, stumbling. Suddenly she felt something small and round beneath her foot. The world spun round—she was falling!

Thump! She sat up and rubbed her eyes. She was sitting on the ground on the other side of the bridge! It had only been a pebble sticking out of the ground.

The old woman glanced back at the sleeping dogs, then ran into a nearby forest. As she went along, the noise of a loom came to her ears. Click clack, clickety clack. She followed the sounds, which led her to a mansion. Its roof was dilapidated and full of holes; rank weeds filled the garden. The old woman crept around back. Wind chimes made of human bones hung under the eaves; stone tubs big enough for a person to sleep in stood about in the yard.

The sounds of the loom continued, click clack, clickety clack. They seemed to come from one of the back rooms. The old woman peeked inside; what did she see but her daughter, sitting alone, weaving. The girl jumped up and ran to her mother, and the two hugged each other for joy.

The girl fed her mother some supper, but just as she was finishing, the thumping of many feet was heard coming toward the house from the forest. The girl hid her mother in one of the big stone tubs, just as a troop of goblins tromped inside. The goblin general stalked about the room, sniffing and snorting and snuffling.

"Why are you sniffing and snorting and snuffling like that?" asked the girl.

"I smell the smell of human flesh," he growled. "Who are you hiding?"

"Oh, don't be silly," the girl replied. "You just haven't gotten used to smelling me. I'm human, after all, and I smell of human flesh."

The goblin general was satisfied with this, and he and his followers sat down for supper. The girl served them food and wine, and as the meal went on the goblins began to get drunk.

Meanwhile, outside, the dogs had smelled the mother hiding in the tub. They walked about the tubs, sniffing, snorting, and snuffling, just as the goblin general had done. One of the goblins went out to see what the trouble was. He stood on the porch and looked over the yard. Everything seemed

normal; only the wind bells of human bones rattled in the evening breeze. The goblin returned to his supper.

A few minutes later the dogs began barking at the stone tub outside the window. Another goblin went out to look, but it seemed normal to him as well.

"They only want some of the food we keep in the tubs," he told the general.

The goblins went on drinking, but the dogs continued to bark. Finally the goblin general sprang to his feet.

"Kill those worthless beasts!" he shouted. "They're giving me a headache!"

Out ran a goblin and killed the dogs, and that was the end of them.

The girl continued to pour wine for the goblins, and soon they began to fall asleep. The general called her to him.

"I'm sleepy," he said. "Put me in the wooden chest with seven lids and seven locks." He often slept in the wooden chest, for it was here that he kept his most precious treasure, and he would count it over as he fell asleep.

The girl helped him to the chest, and at once he fell fast asleep. She closed the seven lids over him, but also locked the seven locks with seven keys. Then she ran past the sleeping goblins out to her mother. She lifted the lid from the stone tub, helped the old woman out, and the two of them ran off to the carriage house.

"Shall we take the cart that goes ten thousand leagues,"

the daughter asked, "or the cart that goes only one thousand?"

Suddenly they heard a voice behind them.

"Take neither one, but take the boat instead." It was the nun, and how she had come there she didn't say.

All three women picked up the boat and made off with it to the river, where they jumped in and began to row across.

Back at the house, the goblin general woke up.

"Girl!" he roared. "I'm thirsty! Get me something to drink!" Again he roared, and again, and again. Still no one came. At last he raised his arms and pushed.

Pop pop pop pop pop pop POP!

Off broke the seven locks and up went the seven lids and out of the chest climbed the goblin general.

"That little bag of human bones escaped!" he yelled to his henchmen. The goblins rubbed their eyes and their heavy heads and ran to the carriage house.

"The cart that goes ten thousand leagues is here!"

"The cart that goes a thousand leagues is here!"

"The boat is gone!"

They all ran down to the river. The boat with the three women inside was little more than a speck in the distance.

"Drink the river dry!" the general ordered. The goblins waded in up to their necks.

Glug glug gurgle gurgle glug glig glug.

They began to gulp down the water.

The river water fell lower, down to the goblins' knees.

The goblins ran out after the boat, the water in their stomachs. Closer, closer and closer they came, until the women could see their fiery red eyes.

"Quick!" cried the nun to the two women. "Do as I do!"

And what did she do but lean right over and show her bare white bottom! The two others followed suit.

Three bare bottoms standing in a rowboat! The goblins had never seen such a sight in their lives. They stopped; they stared. They all burst into giggles. They giggled on, but as they did the river water flowed out of their mouths and filled up the bed of the river. The goblins were left struggling in the middle of the water, while the three women swiftly rowed across to the other side.

There the nun spoke to the old woman.

"I am the spirit of the stone marker you slept on in the field of *susuki* grass," she said. "Please put a new stone there every year; that would make me happier than anything."

With these words, she disappeared.

The mother and daughter returned home to safety. The daughter was soon married to the bridegroom in the village beyond the mountains, where her parents often visited her. And every year thereafter, the mother carefully placed a stone by the marker in the field of rustling grass.

3846